For Jane and Lowdy—*J.D.*
For Rosamund Inglis—*G.P.*

*Indigo and the Whale* copyright © Frances Lincoln Ltd. 1996

Text copyright © Joyce Dunbar 1996

Illustrations copyright © Geoffrey Patterson 1996

First published in Great Britain in 1996 by
Frances Lincoln Limited, 4 Torriano Mews,
Torriano Avenue, London NW5 2RZ

Published in the United States of America by
BridgeWater Books, an imprint of Troll Associates, Inc.

Printed and bound in Hong Kong

10 9 8 7 6 5 4 3 2 1

Library of Congress Cataloging-in-Publication Data

Dunbar, Joyce.
Indigo and the whale / by Joyce Dunbar ; pictures by Geoffrey Patterson.
p. cm.
Summary: Indigo wants to be a musician, not a fisherman
like his father, and with the aid of an enormous whale
he finally gets his wish.
ISBN 0-8167-3802-5
[1. Music--Fiction. 2. Fishers--Fiction. 3. Whales--Fiction.
4. Fathers and sons--Fiction.] I. Patterson, Geoffrey, ill.
II. Title.
PZ7.D8944In 1996
[E]--dc20                                    95-3629

# INDIGO

## AND THE

# WHALE

## JOYCE DUNBAR

Illustrated by

## GEOFFREY PATTERSON

BridgeWater Books

Once there was a boy whose eyes were so blue that his parents named him Indigo. His father was a fisherman, and every morning they went fishing together.

But Indigo wasn't much help to his father. He was too busy playing tunes on an ebony pipe to bother about fishing.

His tame crow loved to listen to Indigo play.

One day, when they were out in the boat, Indigo said to his father, "I don't want to be a fisherman. I'm no good at catching fish. I want to be a musician."

"Stupid boy!" said his father. "You can't earn a living playing tunes. You can't eat music!"

"Perhaps I could make music so wonderful that people would pay to listen to me," said the boy.

His father became angry at this. "I am a fisherman. My father was a fisherman. My father's father was a fisherman. You, too, shall be a fisherman!"

And with that, he snatched the ebony pipe from his son and threw it into the sea.

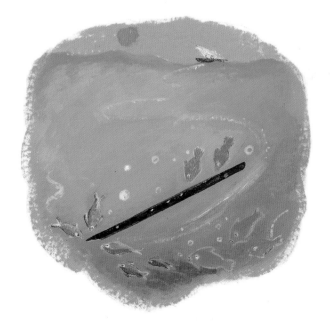

So Indigo could no longer play his tunes. His crow grew sad. Indigo offered him crumbs, but the crow refused to take them.

"Play a tune on your ebony pipe," said the crow. "Then I will want to eat."

"I can't," said Indigo. "My father has thrown it into the sea. He says I must be a fisherman like him."

Soon, Indigo's father fell ill and was unable to take out the boat.

"You will have to go alone," said Indigo's mother. "Otherwise we will starve. Be sure to bring back a good catch."

When the crow heard this, he flew into the forest. He returned with a reed pipe that held all the colors of the rainbow. "This pipe has a special magic," he told Indigo. "Play it at sea to charm your catch and you will never have to go fishing again."

"But I can't fish with a reed pipe," said Indigo.

"Oh yes you can," said the crow, "though you may not be fishing for fish!"

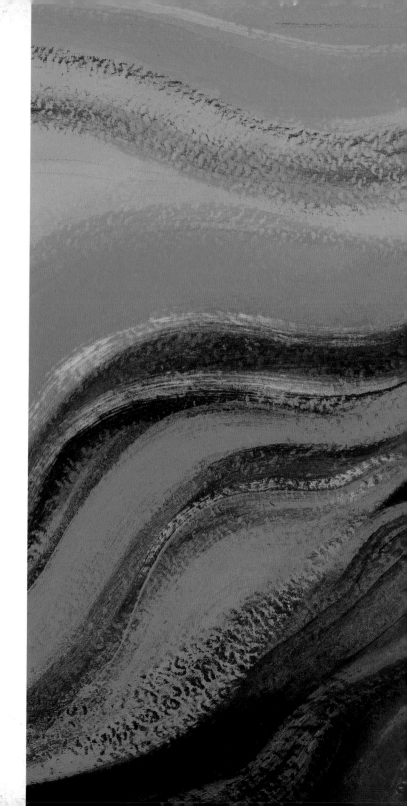

So Indigo followed the crow's advice. He took the boat out on his own. When he was far out at sea he began to play a tune.

A strange shadow appeared underwater. While Indigo played, his boat began to surge through the waves as if carried along by strong currents.

Suddenly a huge creature broke to the surface. It wasn't a fish at all—Indigo had charmed a whale!

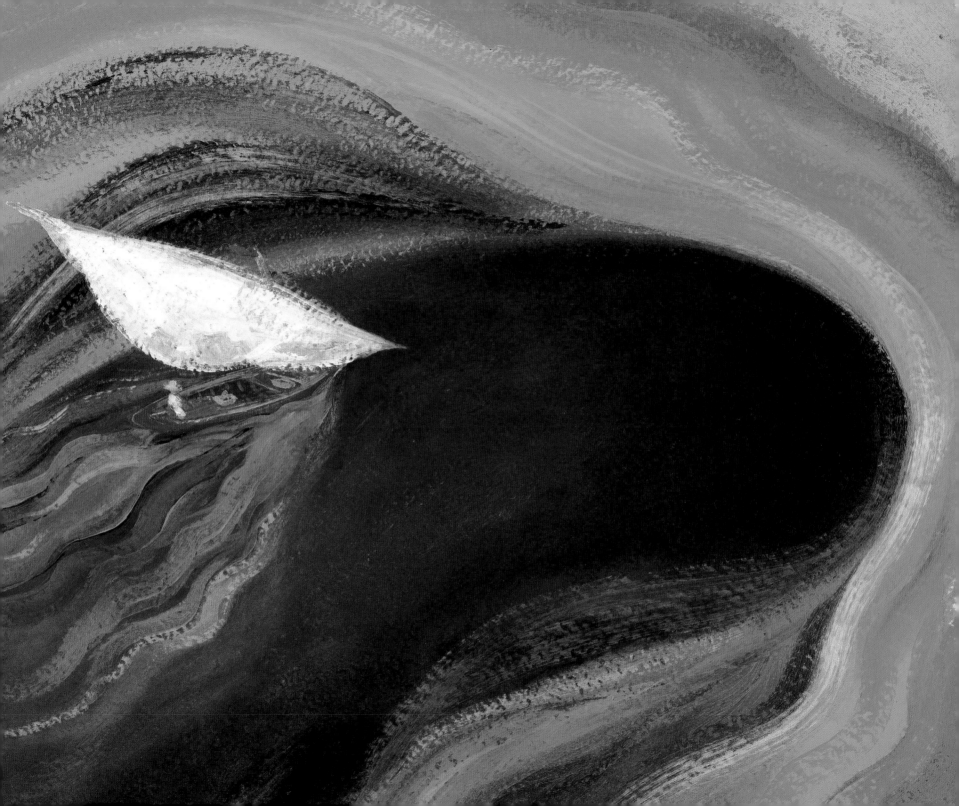

"Please stop your playing," said the whale.

"I won't," said Indigo. "My father is ill and I dare not return without a catch. I must charm you back to the shore."

But when he put the pipe to his lips, the whale dived under the water.

A deep, strange sound began. The whale was singing.
Another whale answered, then another, so that Indigo's
pipe could no longer be heard. Instead, it was his boat
that was charmed, pulled along by the sound of the
whales' song.

The whales sang and swam, sang and swam, until they came to a place where the land was white and the sea was icy cold. Indigo shivered, and his teeth chattered so much that he thought he would freeze to death.

"Now will you stop your playing?" asked the whale.

"No," murmured Indigo. "I will not."

Then the whale began to sing a different song. Another whale answered, then another. Once more, the boat was pulled along. This time they came to a place where the land was parched and dry and the sea was burning hot. Indigo thought he would die of thirst.

"Now will you stop your playing?" asked the whale. "No," panted Indigo. "I will not."

The whale began yet a third song. Other whales
answered. The boat was pulled to the bottom
of the ocean, to its dark, cavernous depths, so that
Indigo could neither see nor breathe. He thought
he was going to drown.

"Now will you stop your playing?" asked
the whale.

"No," gasped Indigo. "I will not."

At this, the whale gave a deep sigh and all the singing stopped. Indigo and his boat shot up to the surface of the water. The whale could no longer resist the charm of the rainbow pipe, and she followed Indigo back to the shore.

The whale made the saddest sound in the world. It seemed as if all the whales were weeping.

"I'm sorry," said Indigo, "but my mother will be so pleased if I take you back to my village. Then I will never have to fish again. I will be able to make music instead."

Silence fell. Then something strange began
to happen. As the life drained out of the whale, so
the colors all around began to fade, until Indigo stood
in a world where everything was gray. Even Indigo's eyes,
which had always been so blue, had turned to gray.
And the world remained utterly silent.

Indigo could find no joy in his music if the whale could no longer make hers. He could feel no pride in such a catch.

"I will stop my playing," he murmured, and he broke the rainbow pipe into pieces.

No sooner had he done this than a great wave rolled up to the shore and carried the whale back out to sea. She began to sing and swim, and all the other whales sang with her. They sang back the colors of the world.

It was the most wonderful music that Indigo had ever heard. Then Indigo saw something at his feet. It was his precious ebony pipe!

Indigo went back to his village. His crow was the first to greet him.

"Now will you play me a tune?" asked the crow. So Indigo put the pipe to his lips and began to play the whale music.

Everyone came to listen. They had never heard such music before. It was filled with all the colors of the world. "Play some more," they begged.

Indigo's father listened too, and his spirits were immediately restored.

"Where did you find such music?" he asked his son.

"At sea, Father," answered the boy.

Indigo's father smiled. "I am a fisherman," he said. "My father was a fisherman, and my father's father was a fisherman. But my son—*he* is a musician!"